Gunn Takes a Gander

A
Barrington Gunn
Caper

by

Nikki Nelson-Hicks

Copyright 2018 © Nikki Nelson-Hicks
Art Copyright 2017© Brenna Gael

ISBN 978-1-7320967-5-2

All rights reserved. No part of this publication may be reproduced, distributed, or transmitted in any form or by any means, including photocopying, recording, or other electronic or mechanical methods, without the prior written permission of the publisher, except in the case of brief quotations embodied in critical reviews and certain other noncommercial uses permitted by copyright law. For permission requests, write to the publisher, addressed "Attention: Permissions Coordinator," at the address below.

No ganders were harmed in the writing of this story.

Any references to historical events, real people, or real places are used fictitiously. Names, characters, and places are products of the author's imagination.

Front cover image by Brenna Gael

First printing edition 2018.
Third Crow Press
640 Bradford Drive
Gallatin, TN 37066

Fiction-

Jake Istenhegyi: The Accidental Detective Series

- ❖ A Chick, a Dick and a Witch Walked Into a Barn- Book 1
- ❖ Golems, Goons and Cold Stone Bitches – Book 2
- ❖ Boodaddies, Bogs and a Dead Man's Booty – Book 3
- ❖ Fished Eyed Men, Fedoras and Steel-Toed Pumps – Book 4
- ❖ Road Trips, Acid Baths, and One Eyed Bastards – Book 5
- ❖ Corpses, Coins, Ghosts and Goodbyes – Book 6

The Astonishing Tales of Sherlock Holmes –The Shrieking Pits

The Galvanized Girl

Gunn Takes a Gander – A Barrington Gunn Caper

The Perverse Muse

A Round for the Holly King

Rumble (Cryptid Clash! Book 5)

What the Armless Guy Said: The Dare Dialogues

Anthologies-

The Adventures of Moose and Skwirl

Capes and Clockwork: Superheroes in the Age of Steam

Legends of New Pulp Fiction

Nashville Noir

Once Upon a Six Gun

Soundtrack Not Included

When the Shadow Sees the Sun – Creatives Surviving Depression

Gunn Takes a Gander

A
Barrington Gunn
Caper

by

Nikki Nelson-Hicks

For Tommy

Bear Gunn sat, sipped coffee and watched a sour man in a beige coat pace angrily across the street. In the man's hands was a yellow piece of paper, an eviction notice, which he twisted as if it were a certain tenant's neck. Bear blew a cooling breath on his coffee and smiled at his landlord, Mr. Steinbaum's annoyance. It was the second one in three months. This wasn't anything serious; it was a game between them. He only had to sit here until his landlord gave up waiting to confront his favorite deadbeat tenant and thumbtack the damn thing into the door so he could tear it off, wad it up and get his day started. He knew Steinbaum loved him. Hell, everybody loved him. Who didn't love Bear Gunn? He was one lovable son of a bitch.

Bear leaned back in the chair and smiled back his best lopsided boyish grin. The one that dropped panties all across Europe a few years ago in the Great War. He was blessed with a head full of curly, honey brown hair and hazel eyes that changed color with his mood. And right now his mood was a bit naughty.

Lillian, the waitress at Rudy's Café sidled up to Bear, wrote out the check and put it down beside him.

"What's this, honey?"

"Your bill. Don't think for a second you're going to skip out on it."

"Lil, my sweet girl, what do you think of me?"

"I think you didn't call me after our date last week."

"Now, hold on, sometimes I get caught up in work and-"

"And I think I saw you with Ruth at the movies two days ago."

"Well, let me just explain myself-"

"And I think you better pay up before I start waving Mr. Steinbaum over."

"Fine, fine!" Bear held his hands up in submission. Steinbaum was walking down the sidewalk, his hands pushed deep in his pockets. Bear watched him pass by the diner. *Ah, the game continues.*

"Lean down here, sweetheart," She complied, and he dug his fingers in her thick russet brown hair, pulled her close and kissed her.

"You really are a bastard," she said, smiling. "You owe me a date."

He ran his fingers around her ears and made a show of pulling out a dime and a nickel out from it. He tossed them down on the table. "Here you go, precious. Now, can I get a piece of your delicious apple pie to go?"

Gunn Investigations was housed in a small office wedged in between a shoe repair and fruit stand. It was drafty, the walls were thin and it stank of the Big Muddy that flowed past the French Market. And that was on a good day. In the summer, the walls would become veined with mold and the flies that collected around Newman's Fruit

Stand would attack and dive into any orifice that came close enough for them to take aim.

Inside, there were two rooms. The first was the reception area. There was a couch, chairs and a small desk where Melinda Page, his secretary, received clients. She was a good bird, a bit of a Dumb Dora when it came to animals, but she worked cheap and was easy on the eyes.

The second room was his office and private sanctum, four walls and a window that opened to an alleyway. He had a simple oak desk, a chair that made obnoxious noises, a sink, a private toilet and a hot plate. Behind the desk were two metal file cabinets: one with a half a dozen case files and the other was a shell that served as a secret hidey hole. Next to the door was a bookcase filled to the brim with *Black Mask* magazines and books by Doyle, Chandler and Hammett, the Holy Trinity of Literature according to Bear Gunn. It was through their words and stories that he rebuilt his life on after the war. If a young man had the good luck to avoid bullets and poisonous gas, then that lucky son of a bitch had better use the rest of his life doing what makes him happy. With that philosophy lodged in his head and an Army pension in the bank, Barrington "Bear" Gunn decided to live the life of his pulp heroes and open up a private detective business.

He tore off the eviction notice, balled it up and unlocked the door. He whistled loudly as he entered.

"Is he finally gone?" Melinda came out of Bear's office. She knew the drill. When Steinbaum came by to collect rent, she hid until Bear gave the all clear. "I was beginning to have palpitations back there."

"Nothing to worry about, doll." Bear threw the paper ball and she caught it, one handed and tossed it back, hitting him square in the forehead. Melinda Page had reflexes like a panther and a wicked right hook. A native of the Crescent City, she was one tough cookie and had more talents than just being able to write short hand. She had saved his ass more than he liked to admit and she enjoyed reminding him of that fact.

"Well, I have good news." Melinda said. "We have a client."

"Oh?"

"Uh-huh. He's still back there in the hidey hole. A real scaredy cat. " Melinda sat down on her desk and crossed her long legs. She liked to wear tight green dresses that showed off her assets much to Bear's approval. She opened up her purse, pulled out her compact and readjusted her tight blond pin curls. She was always fussing with her hair, making sure every twist and twirl was just so. She powdered her cheeks and perky pug nose. "He nearly wet himself when he saw the geese."

Melinda was a magnet for strays. If it slithered, flew or crawled, they somehow found their way to her and, by extension, into his office. It wasn't the first time he had birds in his sink. There have been opossums under the heater, kittens in the cupboard and once she even asked to use one of his beloved *Black Mask* magazines as a liner for a parakeet cage. She learned quickly where Bear Gunn drew the line that day.

"Geez, Mel." Bear pinched the bridge of his nose. "Tell me you aren't keeping birds in my sink."

"Where else do you expect me to keep them?"

"I've told you before that my office is a place of business, not a damn zoo."

"Oh, keep your shorts on, Mr. Big Business Man, it's just until I can get them to Jackson Square. What do you have against geese anyway?"

"I don't like birds." He gave a quick shiver. "They give me the heebie jeebies."

"Don't worry your pretty little head." Mel blew him a kiss. "I'll protect you from the big bad birds."

"Are you going to introduce me to our client? Or should I crack out a damn Ouija board?"

Melinda sighed and closed her mirror with a snap. "For crike's sake! Come out already, you mook!"

"No!" A muffled, squeaky voice shouted. "I'll wait in here."

"See?" Melinda shrugged. "Scaredy cat."

"We'd have ended up back there anyway. Hold my calls, doll."

"Let's see what little old me can do." Melinda took the phone off the hook and laid the receiver on her desk. "Whew. Nearly broke a sweat with that one."

"You know, I could get another skirt."

"Oh yeah, what girl wouldn't love a paycheck that is three weeks late? I'm sure you're beating them off with a stick. I worry myself sick just thinking about it." She pulled out a paper bag from the desk drawer and handed it to Bear. "Would you toss some popcorn to the geese? It's nearly their dinner time."

Bear took the bag and shook his head. *Dames!*

The geese honked up a storm when they saw the door open. How two full grown ganders fit in his sink Bear didn't want to guess.

"Dinnertime, you nasty bastards." Bear reached into the bag and threw a handful of popcorn at them. They caught a few in mid-air, quacking, flapping their wings and spraying water and feathers everywhere.

The door of the faux file cabinet opened and the squeaky voiced man fell out.

"Ahhh! The geese are loose!"

"Settle yourself down, son." Bear helped him up to his feet. "Have a seat."

Gunn tossed the bag and his fedora down on his desk and did a once over on the fidgety little man in front of him. He was mulatto, very light skinned and could probably pass as white in the right light. Young, maybe in his early twenties. His hands were soft and his nails were bitten down to the quick. His hair was chemically straightened like many of the boys who haunted the jazz joints over on Bourbon Street. He had a black eye and he reeked of reefer. His shoes were old but his pants, shirt and jacket were new, recently tailored by the faint blue chalk marks on the pants cuff.

Bear sat down and tallied up his marks: a reefer smoking mulatto who has come into money, probably stolen from someone who wants to make sure this young gentleman doesn't have the time to finish his ensemble with a nice pair of two toned leather Oxfords.

"I'm Barrington Gunn. You saw my name on the door out front. And you are?"

"Jackson Talley. I got your name from some of the boys at the harbor. They said you could help me."

"And what do you want me to do for you?"

"I need you to make me disappear."

Bear laughed. "Not really my area of expertise. Sounds like you need a magician, not a detective. See, I'm more in the business of finding people, not losing them. Sorry, I can't help you."

"My friend, Drake, down at the dock. He said you helped a guy, Bannerman, vanish. Got him a new life."

Bear took a deep breath and exhaled. "Bannerman was a long time ago and a different sort of case. Sorry. I'm not your guy."

The young man shook his head. "No, you don't get it. This is serious deep shinola. If they find me, I'm a dead man."

"What did you do, son?"

"Nothing, sir." Talley rubbed his earlobe and then brushed a hand over his pomade heavy hair.

"Really?" Bear raised an eyebrow.

"I didn't do nothing." Talley started chewing on his thumbnail. "But they think I did."

"Look, I'll give you a piece of advice, okay? On the house. Use the rest of whatever you have left from whatever it is you didn't do and get the hell out of New Orleans."

"You don't think I didn't try? You think I got his shiner shaving? They won't let me leave.

That's why I need to disappear. I've got the money, see?" Talley pulled out a fistful of twenties. "Eighty dollars. It's all I got left and I'll give it to you, all of it, just help me disappear."

Gunn rubbed his chin thoughtfully. Eighty dollars could square the books with Steinbaum and Melinda and even have a few bucks left over for himself.

Gunn took the money, stuffed it in his pants pocket and pulled out a piece of gum. He sat back, unwrapped the Black Jack gum, and started chewing slowly. "You got my help. But I still need to know what I'm getting myself into so, tell me everything and start from the beginning."

Talley let out a huge breath and his shoulders dropped about an inch as the tension left him. "Okay, I'll tell you everything. God's truth, I swear."

"I appreciate that. It makes my job easier when clients don't lie to me."

"I play guitar around town. Not just shine boxes, I've played in white clubs, too. But I got busted for selling a pinch of reefer, lost my gig, and fell on some hard times. I had to hock my strings, and then I got tossed out of my old lady's house so I needed cheap digs to crash. Things were looking down and then I met Joe. I never got his last name. Everybody called him Easy Joe. He and a few friends shared a flat right there in the Quarter and he said I could stay there until I got back on my feet. He said he even had connections, you know, men he worked for who were looking for help. I thought I'd finally found some good luck for once, you know?"

"But these men he set you up with weren't working on the right side of the fence, I bet."

Talley started biting his thumbnail and shook his head. "They'd give us jobs, nothing big time. Just some smash and grabs, nickel and dime stuff. I only intended on staying until I made enough to get my guitar out of hock, you know? Or maybe get a new one."

"Or maybe long enough to get a new suit?" Gunn cracked his knuckles and put his hands behind his head, rocking for a moment as he stared at the water stained ceiling. "Yeah, I got the picture. Forget the particulars and get to what went wrong."

"Joe got picked to do a special job for one of his bosses, Mr. Mallone, a quick smash and grab. Joe said it felt hinky so he asked me to come along."

"Why did it feel hinky?"

"It wasn't the sort of job guys like us were sent on. We're usually just muscle in the back, ya know? And the fact it came from Mallone, well, that put up red flags in my head."

"Why?"

"It wasn't a well-kept secret that Easy Joe and Mallone's favorite girl had a regularly scheduled appointment, if you know what I mean."

"Dames." Gunn shook his head. "It's always dames. What was the job?"

"To break into a house and crack a safe. It was one of those big ones over in the Garden District. Mallone gave us the combination and all the information we'd need: the layout, what kind of security the old broad had, hell, he even knew the damn dog's name."

"What went wrong?"

"What didn't? First, the layout was all screwy and we couldn't find any kind of safe like Mallone said we would. Hell, there wasn't even a dog! But there was a very angry old man who did not appreciate us breaking into his home. He shot Joe twice, right in the gut. Joe shot back, hit the old man right in the forehead. I swear, to God on high, I didn't know Easy Joe was packing heat. A blackjack, a switchblade and some brass knuckles, sure, we both had that stuff but nobody said nothing about bullets."

"Then what did you do?"

"I stood there for a minute, not knowing what to do and then I heard police sirens. Something inside me just took over and I grabbed some stuff that looked expensive enough to hock. I knew once this hit, I'd need to get the hell out of town."

"Why? No one knew you were there."

Talley rubbed his ear. "I got seen. I was bagging the last of the silverware and this old lady caught me in the kitchen. She started pointing and screaming. I rushed out the way I came in but I figured she got a good look at me.

"So, I laid low for a couple of days. Once it seemed okay, I went and hocked my stuff figuring I'd use the money to get a bus ticket and get out of town."

"But first you stopped off to get a new suit."

"I didn't have anything but what I had on my back. Besides, a man needs to look presentable when traveling."

"So why aren't you gone?"

"They jumped me at the bus station."

"Who? Mallone's men?"

Talley shrugged. "I ain't seen these guys before. I just guessed it was but, now that I got time to think about it, it doesn't seem likely. They kept asking me about the box. Where was the box? How would Mallone know about the box?"

"What box?"

"One of the things I stole was a small jewelry box. Well, I thought it was a jewelry box but I never got get it to open. It was dark wood with gold curlicue designs all over it. I got ten dollars for it."

"Where did you hock it? We need to get a better look at this box to see why these men want it so badly."

"Odyssey Shop, over on Magazine."

Gunn picked up his hat. "All right then, let's go."

Talley shook his head. "No, sir. No. I'm not leaving this room. You go yourself, talk to Mama Effie, she runs the joint, and tell her that Talley sent you. She'll talk to you."

"Miss Page said you were afraid of the birds. You okay with them now?"

"I'll take them over whatever is waiting for me out there, sir, thank you."

Gunn stood up, put his fedora on and grinned. "You own my services for as long as your eighty dollars stretches. Feel free to make yourself at home. I'll be back shortly."

He left and closed the door behind him.

"I guess I'm playing babysitter this afternoon?" Melinda said.

"No, doll." He peeled off a pair of ten dollar bills. "Here's your back pay and a little extra."

"Extra?" Melinda took the money, folded the bills and stuffed them in her bra. She arched a perfectly arched brow. "What sort of extra, Mr. Gunn?"

"Research, sweetie, just regular old research. I need you to go and see if there have been any burglaries in the Garden District. Burglaries that went wrong. Like two dead men wrong."

"I have a girlfriend who part times as a police dispatch. She owes me for a bleach job I did for her. She might have some straight dope."

"Good girl, get on that."

"What about our guest? Are we just going to leave him here alone?"

"He's not going anywhere. Scaredy cat, remember?"

"You're the boss. So, where are you going?"

"I've got to go see a woman about a box."

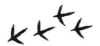

With a few bills in his pocket, Gunn felt a treat was due and hailed a Yellow cab.

"Hello, friend, how much to the Odyssey Shop on Magazine?"

The cabdriver turned his head slowly and chewed on the stub of a cigar like a cow reconsidering its cud. "Around 2 bucks for the drive and another sawbuck not to remember your face should anybody ask."

"Sounds fair. Let's go."

The drive took less than five minutes. Bear got out of the cab, handed over the money and the driver handed him a stained business card:

"Sawbuck Sam, any hour, any parrish. No questions asked. 555-8790."

"Much obliged, Sam." Bear tipped his hat. Sawbuck Sam nodded and drove away. He stood outside the Odyssey Shop. There was a CLOSED sign hanging inside the door. He had heard crazy talk that it was a front for an underworld Mafioso gang that dealt in booze to prostitution and everything they could fit into a hole in between. Bear smirked at the gilded logo above the door, "WE GO TO THE ENDS OF THE EARTH TO SATISIFY YOUR NEEDS!"

Gunn tilted his fedora back and took a peek through the opaque front windows that looked stained from cigar smoke. Inside, it looked like a junk store. Rows and rows of mason jars, knick knacks and all kinds of rubbish. A quick flash of movement alerted him to a woman walking across the floor. She was holding a large book. Gunn knocked on the window, loudly.

She stopped. Her face look distorted through the blurred window. "Go away." she shouted and waved him away. "Can't you read?"

"I need to see Mama Effie. It's important." Gunn said.

The woman came to the door. She was tall, a café colored Creole woman. She looked down on him, and judged him insignificant in a matter of seconds. "Come back tomorrow. We're closed for the day." She pulled down the blind and clicked a bolt closed. "Private affair."

Gunn knocked on the door. "Jackson Talley sent me. About a box."

There was a click as the lock turned and the door opened. The woman was just a wisp, thin as an alley cat, but the sheer force of *HER* filled the entire doorway. All six feet four inches of Bear Gunn shrank away under her gaze. "I am Mama Effie. You have five minutes."

"Thanks."

Bear followed her to the register. She wore a very slinky red dress and a double strand of pearls.

Two bald headed black men dressed in suits sat nearby studiously reading the paper. She sat down in a high backed chair that swiveled and waved her long manicured blood red nails. "Introduce yourself."

"My name is Barrington Gunn. I'm a private investigator."

The two goons made a snorting sound which Bear decided to ignore.

"Jackson Talley was assaulted recently and be believes it may be connected to the box he sold to you. He said it was mahogany with gold inlay, about so big?"

"I have it here." She nodded and pulled the box out from a shelf under the register. It was about as big as a paperback, dark wood with strange symbols etched in gold. It made Bear's eyes hurt to look at it for too long. "It's a puzzle box. My grandmere had one but I can't figure out how to open the blasted thing." She shook it. "Hear that? There is something inside."

"Could be what Talley got his face busted in for. Can I give it a try?"

Mama Effie handed him the box. "I'd be very obliged if you could open it, sir."

Bear held it for a second, feeling the weight. "It's heavy." He turned the box, this way and that, held it up to his eye and squinted. "Yep. It's locked tight. Huh. Let's try this."

He slammed the box, hard, onto the slab gray floor. It split open like a walnut.

"Well, if one wants to get violent," said Mama Effie.

Bear picked it up, put it on the counter and cracked it open. Inside was a smaller golden box.

"Curiouser and curiouser. Look, there's a latch on this one." Bear said as he started to open it.

"Not to quibble but I'd like to remind you that possession is nine tenths of the law." Mama Effie said as she snatched up the golden box. "Ugh, it's leaking." she said and put it back down.

Bear pulled a penknife out of his pocket, opened it and used the blade to flip the latch. He carefully wedged the blade in between the lid, opened it and took a peek.

An eyeball looked back at him.

"What sort of madness is this?" Mama Effie cried out. The two goons shot up from the chairs and ran to her side.

Bear looked closer, poking at the grayish white orb with his penknife. "It looks like inside the gold box was another box, a glass one, that held the eyeball suspended in…" He sniffed the blade. "Smells like pure grain alcohol. Why would anyone want to keep an eyeball?"

"I suppose it depends on who it belonged to." Mama Effie mused. "Either way, I don't want it in my shop. Tell your client he can have it back. He can expect a refund, of course, minus some wear and tear on the merchandise."

"I don't have the power to make that kind of deal." Bear closed the little gold box with its gruesome trinket and slipped it into his pocket. "I'll see what I can do."

Bear took another cab back to the office but this time without the anonymity surcharge. He found Melinda pacing and taking long, nervous drags on a cigarette.

"Uh-oh. What's wrong?"

"Where do you want me to start?" She stamped out the cigarette and lit up another one. "First, our scaredy cat client is gone."

"Gone?" Bear took long strides to his office, opened the door and saw an empty office. "He's gone."

"Is there an echo in here? That's what I said. I'm not blind. I'm just glad the geese are safe."

"Well, as long as they are okay." Bear rolled his eyes as he closed the door. "When are they going to fly the coop?"

"Barb is coming by tonight to get them so don't get your britches in a bunch, okay?"

Bear sat down at Mel's desk. "So, what's got your knickers in a twist?"

"First, tell me this guy has paid his bill in full."

"He did. Cash."

"Good because if half of what I heard is true, I don't think he has time to wait for a check to clear."

"Spill it."

"Officially, there was an incident at a house in the Garden District but written up as vandalism. Unofficially, two bodies were taken to the morgue."

"How can that be unofficial?"

"Because it was at the address of Reverend Du Blanche. Heard of him? No? Well, according to Vicki, Du Blanche is a big roller. He pulls all kinds of strings in local politics, has a pocketful of cops and keeps his fingers sticky with all sorts of creepy, dark mojo. He even claims to have pulled out the eyeball of Marie Laveau to see the future. I ain't saying I believe in any of that sappy, crystal ball, mumbo jumbo but I'm smart enough to know that somebody like brags about plucking out eyeballs is bad news. I'm glad that scaredy cat is gone. We're lucky to be clean of him, if you ask me."

"Well, I don't know how clean we are yet, sweetheart."

Bear pulled the small golden box out and laid it on her desk.

"I'm guessing that's not an engagement ring in that box."

"Don't get your hopes up."

Her pale skin grew a shade greener. "Don't tell me you've got Marie Laveau's eyeball on my desk! Bear, for crying out loud, it's leaking! You're letting voodoo eyeball juice run all over my desk."

"Don't get in a twist, doll." Bear wrapped it in a handkerchief and put it back in his pocket.

"What are we going to do?"

"I've got a plan. We take this back to the owner and ask for a hefty reward. The Reverend gets his eyeball back and we get a double payday. Everything is golden."

"No, no, that's not how this sort of thing goes down, Bear. These people are crazy. It's an eyeball, Bear. *AN EYEBALL.* Do you know what kind of people dig eyeballs out of a dead woman's face? Crazy people, that's who! And worse than that, they are crazy voodoo people. Oh, Bear! They are going to come looking for it and find it here with us and, I don't know! Turn us into zombies? Oh, no…no, they'll turn you into a zombie. I'm too pretty. I'll be sold into white slavery." Melinda held her face in her hands and sobbed, "I don't want to be a voodoo sex slave, Bear!"

"Calm yourself down, woman. How in the world could they possibly track the box to us here?"

A sudden, heavy knock on the door answered him. Melinda cocked a perfectly arched eyebrow.

"That doesn't prove anything. Besides, I don't think they are the kind that would knock."

The knocking continued, louder and heavier.

"Say, you wanna get that, doll? I think that falls under your job description."

"I resign."

The door slammed open and a man stumbled in and landed at Mel's feet. She squealed and kicked him over to reveal a very bloody and battered Jackson Talley.

Bear rushed to the broken man.

"What happened, you damn fool? Why didn't you stay put?"

"I'm so-so-sorry, Mistuh Gunn." Talley sputtered through busted lips. "I didn't think it through."

"They never do, do they?" A smooth baritone said from the doorway. "I guess it is true what they say about help being hard to get these days."

Bear looked up towards the velvety voice. It came from a dark skinned man in a flash midnight blue suit with shiny shoes leaning against the door. He was bald, wore a black eye patch over his left eye and smoked a long white cigarette. He had a ring on each finger. Each ring, Bear mentally calculated would pay his rent for a year.

He looked down at the mush that was Jackson Talley and then back at the Man in the Midnight Blue Suit..

Bear hissed at Mel. "Go to my office. Lock the door. Hide."

For once, Mel did not argue.

"Very good call, Mr. Gunn." He entered the room gracefully like a cat. "I always feel it is best for men to do business without the distraction of beautiful women."

"Well, you have me at a disadvantage." Bear stood, flashed his winning smile and went to meet him. "I don't believe I've had the pleasure of meeting you."

"Ah, forgive my rudeness. It has been a busy day. First, my colleagues were lucky to find Mr. Talley at his favorite reefer peddler's. After some coercion, he confessed that he stole something precious from me. A box about so big but he had sold it to the Odyssey Shop. So, then we had to go all the way to Magazine Street. The lady of the shop was a tad hesitant but I am very persuasive. She gave me this."

Midnight Blue Suit tossed the broken box to Bear.

It was sticky with blood and Bear felt his face grow hot.

"I'm the most honorable Reverend Henri Du Blanche and owner of the contents of that box."

"It's empty."

"So it is."

"So, to me, it looks like you're the owner of jackshit."

"Ah, that is where I hope you could be of assistance."

"Me?" Bear tightened his grip on the box.

"You find things, yes?" Du Blanche said as he moved in closer. Bear saw two great hulking men in suits come in and close the door.

"Sometimes."

"Then, let's be professional. I want to hire you to find what was in that box. And, to be completely frank with you, I believe this will be an exceptionally easy job for you."

"Do you?"

"Yes, since I believe you already know where it is and most importantly," Du Blanche lifted up the eye patch to show Bear the gaping, red empty eye socket, "what it is."

Bear swallowed down a wad of bile. "That looks nasty. Have you seen a doctor? Could be infected."

He replaced the eye patch. "Stop playing stupid. The woman at the shop screamed your name as I was cutting into her face." Bear's face reddened and his nostrils flared. Du Blanche smiled and took a step closer. "Speaking of pretty faces, where is your woman?"

"Leave her out of this."

He snapped his fingers and his goons came to his side. "Perhaps she knows something."

"Don't you even think about it, bud. I'm warning you."

"No! I won't let you hurt her, too." Talley got to his feet and grabbed Du Blanche, pulling on his arm. "I won't let you."

"Get off me, pig!" Du Blanche slapped the pitiful man. Talley went down in a heap and the goons went to work kicking and punching him to make sure he stayed down.

"That's it!" Bear exploded and decked the first goon with a haymaker that sent teeth flying across the room. "Leave the poor son of a bitch alone! Try taking me on for size!" The second goon reached for his gun but Bear pulled him in close for a jab and grab, pulled the gun away and pistol whipped him until he fell unconscious. Huffing and red faced, he turned to go at Du Blanche who stood calmly to the side, holding a .38 with his finger on the trigger.

"If we're finished playing, shall we do business?"

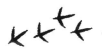

Bear tossed Talley over his shoulder and took him back to his office. Du Blanche and his men followed behind. He carefully put the unconscious man down in his chair.

The geese honked and flapped at the sight of him and begged for dinner. Bear picked up the bag and tossed a few popcorn kernels at the birds. He grabbed a handful more and stashed it in his coat pocket.

"Filthy birds." Du Blanche grimaced and swatted at the down that floated in the air. "Where is the woman?"

Bear shrugged. "Maybe she went out the window? Who knows when it comes to dames?"

"Let's get down to business. Do you have Laveau's Eye?"

Bear sat on the corner of his desk and thrust his hands deep in his coat pockets. "Yep."

"Give it to me."

"Whoa, son, perhaps you don't understand the fundamental concept of a free market. See, it goes like this: I have something you want, you pay me and then I give it to you. I think you forgot about that second bit. You look like the sort that carries a big wad so I'm thinking about a five hundred dollars is a good going rate."

Du Blanche nervously rubbed the stones on his rings. "Show me first."

"A show of good faith? You catch on quick." Bear took the handkerchief out of his pocket. He unfolded it and held up the golden box. "See?"

"Open it."

"You hurt my feelings, sir. I don't think you trust me."

"I don't. Show me the Eye and then I'll give you the money."

"Okay, the customer is always right." Bear started to stand but slid awkwardly off the desk and toppled forward, the handkerchief flying up.

"Dinnertime!" He said as he reached out with his other hand, tossing popcorn everywhere.

"SQUAWK!" The geese responded to the dinner bell, flapped their wings and snatched up the kernels and the white handkerchief in midair. They gobbled and fought over each bit until only the stained, white cloth remained.

"No!" Du Blanche screamed. He started chasing the birds that flew around the room, deftly avoiding the raging man and sailed out the window.

Du Blanch pounded his fists on the window sill, "Damn you! Damn you to hell!"

"Bad luck!" Bear came up behind him and slapped him on the shoulder. "You'd best get after them. I'd try Jackson Square. I hear birds love that place."

"You bastard! Do you know what you cost me?"

"I don't know about you but I'm out 500 big ones."

"You stupid son of a bitch." Du Blanch snapped his fingers. "Kill him!"

Gunn Takes a Gander

The beaten and battered goons swaggered up to Bear.

"Oh, now, boys, are you sure you're ready for another round with me?"

The goon on the left pushed his broken nose back into place and spit out a wad of blood. "Yeah, sure. I think I got my second wind back. How about you, Des?"

The one on right nodded, pulled out a blackjack and slapped it against his beefy palm. "I got your back, Harry."

"Okay, okay. You got me." Bear put his hands up and pointed behind them. "But how about her?"

Melinda was standing behind them with two .38 revolvers, the hammers pulled back, her finger on both triggers, pointed at their backs. "Hello, boys. Miss me?"

"I'm not afraid of a woman." Du Blanche sneered..

Melinda swerved a few degrees to the left, pulled the trigger, shot the window sill beside Du

Blanche's hand and was back on point in seconds flat. "You should be."

"Her typing sucks but, man, oh man," said Bear. "She can hit a fly off a cow's tit."

Du Blanche spit in Bear's face "This is not over, Mr. Gunn. Mark my words, you have made a terrible enemy today."

Bear pulled the handkerchief out of Du Blanche's pocket, wiped his cheek and handed it back to him. "So, should I add the geese to the bill?"

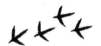

Later that evening, Mel met with Bear at Rudy's Café.

"Will the scaredy cat be okay?" she asked.

"He's pretty banged up. I left him at the hospital." Bear laughed. "Told them to bill the Most Honorable Reverend Henri Du Blanche."

"You shouldn't laugh. I think you are going to pay dear for today's little shenanigans."

"Maybe." Bear stirred his coffee. "Sorry about the birds, Mel."

"Geese are geese. There will always be more. I'm sorry it cost us a payday."

"Did it?"

Mel's eyes went wide. "What did you do?"

"Let's just say I have very nimble fingers. A quick bit of misdirection and, voila!" He fanned out his hands, clapped and produced a small golden box.

"Bear…is that?"

He flashed a smile. "Know anybody in the market for one magic eyeball, gently used?"

The End

Nikki Nelson-Hicks has the great honor of being described as "the unholy lovechild of Flannery O'Connor and H.P. Lovecraft."

She is the author of Jake Istenhegyi: The Accidental Detective series available on Amazon.com where the character of Bear Gunn is a heavy hitter.
Visit amazon.com/author/nikkinelsonhicks for more titles.

Made in the USA
Middletown, DE
17 September 2024